KITTY...
A Cat's Diary

Written by Robyn Supraner
Illustrated by Diane Paterson

Troll Associates

Library of Congress Cataloging in Publication Data

Supraner, Robyn.
   Kitty—a cat's diary.

   Summary: A cat writes in her diary about the first
year with her new master, a playful and affectionate
boy.
   [1. Cats—Fiction]   I. Paterson, Diane, 1946-   ill.
II. Title.
PZ7.S9652Ki   1986   [E]   85-14023
ISBN 0-8167-0574-7 (lib. bdg.)
ISBN 0-8167-0575-5 (pbk.)

KITTY...
A Cat's Diary

September 10

Dear Diary:

This is my lucky day! I found
a boy. His name is Dennis and
he has a nice face. His mother
says I can stay. So it's goodbye
to garbage pails and hello to the
good life!

September 15

Dear Diary:

Dennis forgets I'm a cat. Like last night—he said, "Hey, Kitty, let's play submarine." Guess who was the submarine?

8

October 6

Dear Diary:

Today at school I was the star of Show and Tell. The dress didn't look too bad. But stockings? P.S. I won first prize.

October 17

Dear Diary:

We're buddies! We're partners!
We're friends to the end!

P.S. Did you ever ride a bike?

October 31

Dear Diary:

Today is Halloween. We
dressed up in our scariest
costumes. I got a chocolate bar,
ten jellybeans, four cookies, and
a dime for trick-or-treat.

November 13

Dear Diary:

Today we played Cops and Robbers. I was the Robber. I hope I get out of jail soon!

November 26

Dear Diary:

Today is Thanksgiving. I am thankful for Dennis, and he is thankful for me.

P.S. I had some turkey.

December 5

Dear Diary:

It snowed! Today we went sledding. Do you think some cats have more than nine lives?

18

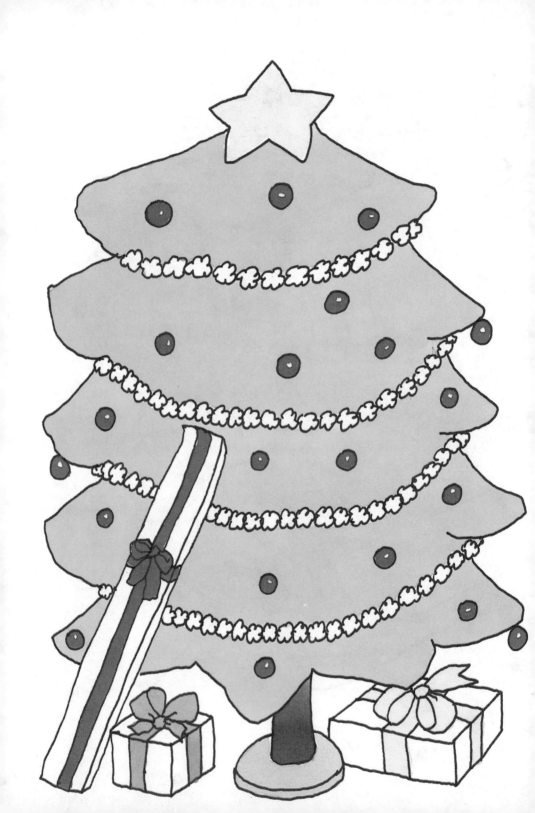

December 25

Dear Diary:

We strung popcorn and hung it on a tree. Everybody got presents. I gave Dennis a mouse. He gave me skis!

P.S. Merry Christmas!

December 26

Dear Diary:
I went skiing!

December 27

Dear Diary:
 I went skiing again—I'm
tired!

December 31

Dear Diary:

We had balloons and confetti and everything! At twelve o'clock we banged on pots and pans. The baby sitter put us to bed five times. Happy New Year!

24

January 12

Dear Diary:

   More snow. Dennis' father
made a fire in the fireplace. We
all sang songs and drank hot
chocolate. It was very cozy, but
I never did like marshmallows!

February 14

Dear Diary:

Dennis and I baked a Valentine cake. It had three layers. It had sprinkles and a whole jar of cherries. Everyone took a bite. Dennis' father said, "One bite is enough!"

February 21

Dear Diary:

We went ice-skating today. It certainly was exciting.

March 23

Dear Diary:

It rained and rained all day.
Dennis and I went to the
movies. I didn't get to see the
whole show.

April 10

Dear Diary:

Today I met Jingles! He's got the longest whiskers and the most beautiful tail. I giggle when he purrs!

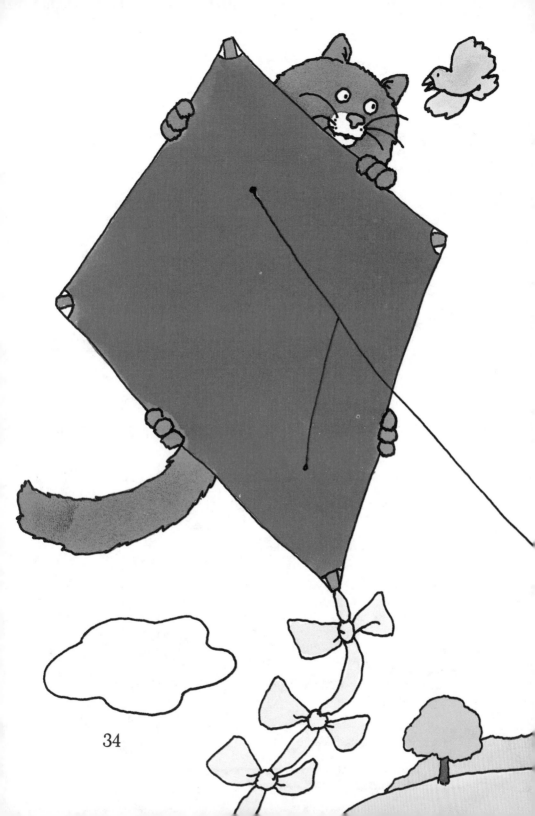

April 20

Dear Diary:

We flew kites today. The
house looks different from up
there in the sky. I had a chat
with a very friendly sparrow.

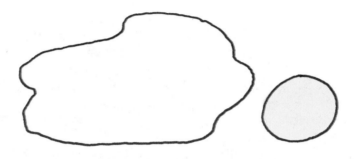

35

May 19

Dear Diary:
Someone should buy a basket
for Dennis' bicycle. It would
make me very happy—especially
when we go downhill!

June 1

Dear Diary:

Jingles came calling this morning at 3 A.M.! He sang to me. Oh, Diary, he has such a beautiful voice!

P.S. The neighbors didn't think so.

Dear Diary:

Dennis' parents bought a plastic swimming pool. It looks pretty deep. Dennis is buying me water wings. What *are* water wings?

June 30

Dear Diary:
   I found out what water wings
are!

July 1

Dear Diary:
I'm tired!

42

Dear Diary:

Dennis and I marched in the parade. I didn't mind the flag on my tail, but I'll never learn to play the harmonica!

Dear Diary:

I've got a surprise! It's a
wonderful present! I think it
will be ready for Dennis'
birthday!

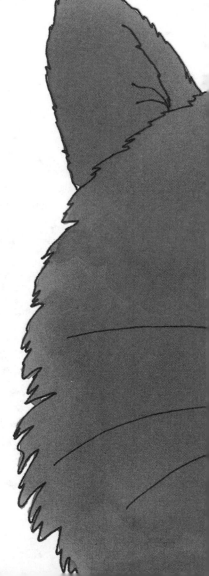

August 3

Dear Diary:

We all went to the beach. I didn't go in the ocean. I stayed under the umbrella.

Dear Diary:

It's Dennis' birthday! We had ice cream and cake and a lot of presents. Dennis got a football and crayons. He got a robot and an airplane. But he liked my present best of all!